JUST PLAIN BOB

I0547720

Leslie's KINKS

EROTIC SEXUAL DISCOVERIES

WARNING

This book contains sexually explicit scenes and adult language. It may be considered offensive to some readers. This book is for sale to adults ONLY.

Please store your files wisely where they cannot be accessed by underage readers.

* * * * * * * * * * * * * * * * * * *

About the Publisher

4Fun Publishing, a member of **BLVNP Incorporated**, 340 S. Lemon #6200, Walnut CA 91789, info@blvnp.com / legal@blvnp.com

NOTE: Due to the highly emotional reaction of some people to works of erotic fiction, any email sent to the above address that contains foul language or religious references is automatically deleted by our anti-spam software and will not be seen. All other communications are welcome.

DISCLAIMER

Leslie's Kinks
Erotic Sexual Discoveries

By: Just Plain Bob

© **Just Plain Bob 2015**
ISBN: 978-1-68030-512-8

CHAPTER 1

I should have known better than to get into an argument with my wife. Past experience has shown that she will go to extremes to win, even if she ends up biting off her nose to spite her face, and that's just what happened here.

Leslie is an outspoken woman and she has an opinion on everything under the sun. Those opinions are strong and forceful and for the sake of peace and harmony I've learned to keep my mouth shut since I have never been able to change her mind on anything. The latest brouhaha came about at a cocktail party that her company was throwing for its customers. We were at a table in the center of the room and I noticed a tall, good looking black man circulating through the crowd and greeting people. I also noticed that while he had visited every table around us, he had not even glanced our way. I asked Leslie who he was and she told me that his name was Tony and he was the head of accounting. When I mentioned that he seemed to be avoiding our table she said, "That's not surprising. He knows that I don't care for him."

"Why not?" I asked. "He seems to get along with everyone else here."

She glanced in his direction and said, "He is an arrogant son of a bitch and I just don't like him."

I chuckled and said, "You don't like him because he's black," and the minute I said it, I knew that I'd fucked up.

"And just what do you mean by that?" she demanded.

Well, once I take Leslie on I won't back off any more than she will so I said, "You know full well what I mean. You have a prejudice against blacks, it shows when you are around them and it makes them uncomfortable so they avoid you." This was a subject that I definitely should have avoided because she immediately got her back up.

"Bull! Give me one instance when I've shown prejudice against blacks," and I began ticking them off one by one on my fingers while she kept interrupting me to "explain" why she had done this, that, and the other.

"Okay," I said "Go ahead and get Tony and bring him over to the table. Tell him you would like him to meet your husband."

She scowled at me. "No! I don't have to prove anything to you. I am not prejudiced!"

I should have just let it go, but I didn't. There were about six or seven blacks at the party and so I said to her, "Okay, let's go over and sit with them" and I pointed at a table where two black couples were sitting. But she had an excuse why we couldn't go sit with them so I pointed at another couple that was sitting alone. She said no to that too. "Face it, Leslie, you are a bigot."

Now she was mad and she practically hissed at me, "No, I am not!"

"Okay," I said. "Prove to me that you are not."

She asked me how she could do that and I thought for a minute and then I said, "Ask Tony to lunch. Tell him that you sense that the two of you seem to be uncomfortable around each other and you thought that maybe you could sit down and discuss it over lunch. In the interest of work place solidarity and stuff like that."

She took the dare. "Okay, I will!" I sat there watching her and waiting for her to get up and go over to him, but she didn't. Finally she said, "What are you looking at?"

I smiled and said, "Just waiting."

"For what?" she wanted to know.

"For you to go ask him."

She gave me a nasty look. "I am not going to do it tonight. I'll do it at work tomorrow. It will be more natural."

I smiled to myself and made myself a bet that it would never happen.

Next night at dinner I asked Leslie how her lunch with Tony went and she told me that she had gotten so busy that she'd not had a chance to ask him. I kept on her about it for the next two or three weeks, asking her two or three times a week about her lunch with Tony, and I always got the same answer, she was just too busy to get around to it. Finally I said, "Leslie, just admit you are prejudiced against blacks."

"I am not!"

I grinned at her and said, "You are until you prove to me that you're not."

After that I stopped getting on her about Tony and nothing more was said until her company Christmas party. When we arrived I noticed that there were empty seats at the table where Tony was sitting and I pointed to the table and said, "Let's sit there."

She shook her head and said, "No. I don't want to sit there."

I chuckled and said, "I knew you would say that."

She gave me a nasty look and hissed, "Damn you! I am not a bigot!" and then she took me by the arm and led me to a different table. I decided to shut up on the subject and just sit back and enjoy the party, but about an hour and a couple of drinks into it Leslie said, "You still think I'm prejudiced, don't you?"

I shrugged and said, "I know you are."

She looked me right in the eye and said, "What do I have to do to prove you wrong?"

This should be fun, I thought, and I began looking around the room for what I hoped would be there, and there it was, down near the end of the bar. "Tell you what," I said. "There are eight black guys here tonight. You dance with any three of them, or get one of them under the mistletoe" and I pointed to the end of the bar, "and kiss him and I'll never mention it again."

Leslie gave me a look that said as plain as any words could have, "You'll pay for this!"

Three or four drinks later Leslie got up and started to circulate and she finally ended up at a table where a black couple and a single black man were sitting. A few minutes later the single man got up and escorted Leslie out onto the dance floor. The band was playing a slow waltz and Leslie moved in close to the man and over his shoulder she shot me a glance that said, "Fuck you!"

When the dance was over she went back to the table with the man and sat down and had a drink with them. A few minutes later she got up with the other man and they moved out onto the dance floor. Again, it was a slow one and she moved close to the man and I saw his hand slide down to her ass. This should get interesting, I thought, and I waited for her to slap him or at least pull away, but she didn't. I did see her look my way to see if I was watching, and I could tell that she was planning on teaching me a lesson (I'll teach you to doubt me, damn you).

Back to the table with the man after the dance and another drink with them and then a white guy asked her to dance and then one or two more and then another black guy, which gave her the three I'd challenged her to. But she wasn't through putting me in my place yet. She came over to our table and said, "Come on. We're going to join them."

When we got over to their table, they had put five tables together and we ended up with twenty-three people sitting there, including two more black men, one of whom was Tony. More drinks and pretty soon Leslie had danced with every guy at the table except Tony. I was being social and I was dancing with the wives and girlfriends of the guys at the table, and outside of an occasional dance with Leslie I wasn't paying much attention to her anymore. She had already danced with every black man there (except Tony) thereby proving to me that she was not a bigot (even though I knew she was - all she'd done was take a dare).

I was dancing with Sylvia, the girl friend of one of the guys at the table, and she said to me, "You seem like a nice guy. Can I ask you something?"

"Sure," I said. "Go ahead."

"What's your wife trying to prove tonight?"

I looked down at her and said, "I don't know what you mean."

Sylvia said, "For three years, as long as I've been with the company, she has gone out of her way to avoid minorities. Tonight all of a sudden, she's dancing with them and has even gotten kissed under the mistletoe by a few."

That surprised me, as I hadn't seen it. "Maybe she is just trying to correct some misconceptions," I said.

"Bull shit!" she fired back. "I've been watching you watch her all night and there is something going on and I'm a curious kitten. I want to know what it is."

I probably should have ignored her question, but I'd had just enough booze in me to loosen me up and I kind of liked Sylvia so I told her. Sylvia said, "How about you? You got any prejudice in you?"

I smiled at her. "None that I am aware of."

She smiled back and said, "Prove it. Dance me over to the mistletoe and kiss me."

I took it as a dare and I waltzed her over to it and bent to give her a brief kiss on the lips, but her hands came up and held my head as she pushed the tip of her tongue in to my mouth and I slipped my tongue into hers. What was supposed to be a brief peck on the lips turned into something very, very steamy. Sylvia broke the kiss and gave me a strange look. "We'd better get back to the table," she said.

"Why? The music is still playing?"

She grinned. "I know, but doing a waltz with you while you have that lump in your pants would be difficult for me," and I suddenly became aware that I did indeed have a stiffy. I think I might have blushed because Sylvia giggled and took my hand and led me back to the group. For the next half-hour or so Sylvia sat next to me, talked with me and teased me unmercifully. Finally she reached over and squeezed the lump in my pants (her teasing had kept me hard) and asked, "Have you figured it out yet?"

I gave her a questioning look and she said, "Have you figured out what's going on?"

I shrugged and said, "What?"

"Why I'm teasing you?" I looked at her and she said, "Look around. What do you see?" I looked around the room, but I couldn't pick up on what she after so I looked back at her and shrugged again. "What you don't see is your wife. She hasn't been here for over half an hour."

I took another look around and did not see Leslie so I turned back and asked her what she was trying to tell me. I had trouble believing what she told me, but the fact was that Leslie wasn't in the room. Apparently Leslie's attitude at the party had registered on the black guys (and some whites) and they couldn't figure out the sudden change in her. They got together and decided to see if they could make it work to their advantage. The black guys had each thrown fifty bucks into a pot and it was winner take all. To be the winner all you had to do was be the first guy to fuck Leslie. And there was more. There were several side bets between some of the white guys and the black guys on whether or not it could be done. The white guys were betting that the black guys couldn't, while hoping that they could, because if the black guys could then the white guys thought they would have a shot at making her.

"My job was to keep you occupied so they could work on hustling your wife."

The tone of her voice when she said that made me look at her. "Do you hate her that much?" I asked.

"You bet. She passed me over for a promotion even though I was the most experienced and best qualified. The only thing I had going against me was the color of my skin."

"So why are you telling me this now?" I wanted to know.

She stroked my cock again and said, "Two reasons. She and Tony have been gone for long enough for him to have done the deed, and I want a touch of revenge for myself. I want to fuck her husband." She gave my dick another squeeze. "And he just might be willing now that he knows what his wife has been up to."

My cock gave an involuntary twitch when Sylvia said that and she giggled. "Was that because you want a taste of my brown sugar, or is it because the thought of a black cock sliding into your wife is a turn on?"

To be honest about it, I think it was a little bit of both.

It was another twenty minutes before I saw Leslie walk back into the room and about five minutes later Tony came in. I looked closely at Leslie but I couldn't see anything that would tell me one way or the other if she had done anything or not. I danced the next dance with her.

"Having fun?" I asked.

She tucked her head into my shoulder and said, "I'm having a blast. I'm really glad we came."

Over her shoulder back at the table I saw one of the guys hand Tony a wad of money. When the dance was over we went back to the table and Leslie had another drink and a few minutes later a guy asked her to dance. While she was out on the floor I leaned over to Sylvia and said, "I saw one of the guys hand Tony a bunch of money. Does that mean what I think it means?"

She grinned at me and asked, "How bad do you want to find out?"

I asked her what she meant and she said, "If she did and I give you my phone number, will you call?"

Why not, I thought, what did I have to lose? Over the next half-hour I danced with a few other wives and girlfriends and I saw Tony dancing with Sylvia. I also saw Leslie under the mistletoe with one of the black guys and it was no peck on the lips that she was getting (or giving). I noticed the guy had a hand on her ass and their loins seemed to be pressed together, but I couldn't be sure about that from my angle. A minute or so later I saw Leslie leave the ballroom and a minute or so after that the guy she had been kissing went out. When the band took a break I walked the woman I had been dancing with back to the table and then I went and sat down beside Sylvia. I gave her an inquiring look and she said, "Are you sure you want to hear this? Knowing could be a bitch. You could just let it go and write it off to me bad mouthing her because I don't like her."

I told her that I wanted to know and she said okay, but remember our deal and she handed me a piece of paper with her phone number on it. I remembered our agreement and I folded the paper and put it in my pocket. "He did her on the back seat of your car. It took him almost a half an hour to get her there, but he said it was worth it."

Until then I wasn't sure that anything I'd heard from Sylvia might be true, but I had seen Leslie come in followed by Tony and I'd just seen her leave followed by another black man. A black man who I'd just seen her in a passionate embrace with.

"Would Tony lie about something like that?"

"Honey, Tony is my brother and we tell each other everything. He doesn't lie to me and I don't lie to him. If he said he got into your wife's panties, he did!"

I was quiet for a minute and then asked, "Does he know that you're telling me this?"

She laughed at me and said, "Honey, I told you we tell each other everything. I told him how you dared her to prove she wasn't a bigot and he told me that you can find all the proof you need on the center of the seat on the right side of the back seat in your car."

I sat there in silence because I didn't have any idea of what to say and then she said, "There is more, if you want to hear it." I nodded at her to go ahead. "Tony doesn't think she's spread for anybody else yet, but she has been doing some pretty heavy necking with some of the guys and she has given out one hand job that Tony knows about. He thinks she has sucked the cock of another, but he's not sure."

The image of the guy following Leslie out of the ballroom flashed through my mind.

"I'll tell you the whole story, honey, word for word, move by move of what the two of them did and what Tony finds out from the other guys, but only after you call me."

I gave her a weak smile and then concentrated my attention on the ballroom entrance. Thirty minutes later Leslie came back in and the man who had followed her out came in about a minute or so behind her. If there had been any doubt in my mind over whether Sylvia had been telling me the truth, it was gone now.

As the evening drew to a close I kept asking myself what I should do, how I should handle the situation. On the one hand I had every reason to believe that my wife had been unfaithful to me, possibly several times. On the other, I had egged her into it; pushed her into the situation that made it happen. I knew she would go to any lengths to win an argument with me, but I'd no idea she would go that far. What if I did say something and all she did was some necking? All I had to go on was seeing her leave the room and come back and what Sylvia had told me, and Sylvia did not like Leslie and didn't bother to hide it. I decided to keep quiet and see what Leslie had to say.

We got in the car to leave and Leslie slid over next to me like she used to when we were teenagers. She reached over and placed her hand on my cock and said, "I really, really hope you are in the mood tonight, honey, because I'm hot enough to fuck a whole bunch of guys."

Interesting way to put it, I thought, especially since I already suspected that she might have done just that.

She reached over and took one of my hands and put it between her legs. "Feel how wet I am," and she was definitely that. I also noticed that she didn't have her panties on and I mentioned it. "That's because I wanted your fingers in me on the way home."

"What made you so horny?" I asked.

"Haven't you been watching me tonight? Damn near every guy there got me under the mistletoe and most of them felt me up when they kissed me." She giggled. "I got even with some of them. I squeezed their cocks while they had their hands on my ass." She giggled again. "I never realized the guys I work with could be so much fun."

I wondered what she really meant when she said that. "Do you still think I'm a racist?"

I glanced at her and said that she did what I'd asked her to do and I had no intention of mentioning the matter again.

"Yes, baby, but I could have just been taking a dare. What if I told you that I did something on my own, something you didn't tell me I had to do?"

Sweet Jesus, I thought, she really did do it and now she's going to rub my face in it. I concentrated on keeping my shaking hands gripped tight on the steering wheel and she said, "Yep! I did something on my own. I'm having lunch with Tony tomorrow."

Damn, does that mean she's going to fuck him again? When we got home and I was getting out of the car, I glanced at the back seat. In the center of the right side of the seat was a spot that hadn't been there that morning. As I shut the car door I remembered the slip of paper that Sylvia had given me. I reached into my pocket to make sure I still had it.

***

Leslie was very wet and I was certain that it was someone else's cum and not, as she tried to tell me, her own juices. The one thing I did know for sure is whatever had happened at the party that night, it had turned Leslie into a sex maniac. Our sex life was usually limited to three or four times a week and then usually only one time, but that night she would not leave me alone. As soon as we got into the bedroom she pulled me to the bed and we did it with our clothes still on. When I came we undressed and she sucked me hard again, pushed me back on the bed and mounted me. I came the second time and she went to work on me again. The more she fucked me, the more I had to know what had happened to her at the party, and the only way I was going to find that out was call the number that Sylvia had given me. I made up my mind to do it the first thing next morning.

The next day I called Sylvia and asked her to lunch. She laughed. "Curiosity killing you?" and I admitted that it was. "Okay, baby, but it's going to cost you more than lunch."

"What exactly do you have in mind?" I wanted to know.

"Honey, it means that you are springing for lunch, but I get to pick the dessert."

We met at a small café and Sylvia got right to the point. "I'll tell you everything that Tony told me, but my price is still what I said it would be the other night. I want my revenge. I'm not going to broadcast it, but whenever I look at her I want to be able to smile and say to myself 'Hey bitch, I've fucked your husband'."

I just sat there and looked at her while I tried to figure out what to say.

"What's the matter? You don't want to know bad enough to dip your white wick into some black girl?"

I laughed at her and said, "Do you know how stupid that sounds? A good looking and very sexy lady trying to blackmail a guy into going to bed with her? I'm a little hesitant because I've never cheated on my wife and I never expected that I would."

Sylvia smiled and said, "Sugar, she did it first and as far as I'm concerned that releases you from whatever vows you may have taken."

She was right and so I said, "I agree to your conditions. Tell me what happened."

The story was simple enough. Leslie had taken my challenge and had gone out to prove me wrong. By the time the night was half over she had managed to dance with every black man there, and had gotten every one of them under the mistletoe, except Tony. For some reason he wouldn't ask her to dance so she took the bull by the horns and asked him. Halfway into the dance she asked him why he hadn't tried to get her under the mistletoe like everyone else had. Tony asked her why he would want to do something like that and Leslie had answered that she wanted it. Tony gave her a long look and then maneuvered her to the end of the bar. Tony gave her a long kiss, with a little tongue, and Tony responded by slipping her a little back. It was a kiss that lasted a good ten or so seconds and when they broke apart Tony had given her another long look and then had asked her what had gotten into her that night. Leslie told him the truth. That she had been perceived as a racist and she was trying to disprove it.

"So you aren't doing this on your own, you are just trying to prove something to someone."

Leslie said that wasn't true and Tony said that yes it was. That she was dancing and doing the mistletoe thing because someone was watching her do it. Leslie protested and said he was wrong and Tony had taken her by the hand and had led her from the ballroom. Leslie wanted to know where he was taking her and Tony said he was taking her to some place where they couldn't be seen. When they were alone he said, "Okay, now kiss me while there is no one around to applaud your liberalism."

Leslie stood on tiptoe and kissed him. She gave him tongue and he gave some back. The kiss was a hot one and lasted quite a bit. When they broke they stood looking at each other for several seconds and then Tony bent his head to kiss her again and she went up on tiptoe to meet him half way. That kiss was as hot or hotter than the first one and they were both breathing hard when they broke apart. They were silent for a minute and then Tony told her that she hadn't proven anything.

"You just took my dare. You have to do something on your own, something that no one told you to do, something that no one else would ever know about."

Leslie had looked at him and said, "Like what?" and Tony had said, "No way, lady. No input from me or anyone else. It's got to be something that you do on your own."

Leslie had looked into Tony's face for several moments and then she had reached for his zipper. She wrestled out his cock and then went to her knees and took him in her mouth and started to suck his cock. After a few minutes she stopped and looked up at him. "Proof enough?" and Tony had told her that the only thing she had just proved was that she was a heartless bitch to take him that far and then quit. Leslie got mad and said, "What do you want? To take me here on this cement floor?"

And Tony had said, "No, the back seat of your car would be fine."

Leslie had given him an exasperated look and then she laughed. "You're right. It wouldn't be right for me not to finish what I started," and she took him by the hand and led him to our car. She had fucked him once and then had sucked him hard again and let him fuck her a second time.

When they had finished and they were getting out of the car Tony had said, "There are a couple of others who might like you to show them you're not a bigot," and he pointed to two black men leaning against the wall smoking.

Leslie had laughed and said, "You're not going to be happy until you get me gang fucked, are you?"

Tony smiled and said, "Not a bad idea and I'll bet it would be fun."

I sat and listened to Sylvia tell me the story that Tony had related to her and I could see it happening that way. Basically Tony had goaded her the same way I had and she had responded the same way she had to me - the old "I'll show you" attitude. "What about the others you told me about, the blowjob and the hand job?"

Sylvia smiled and said, "You sure are a glutton for punishment."

According to Tony, who saw Leslie give the hand job, one of the guys who had been leaning against the wall had approached Leslie and offered to keep quiet if she would take care of him. She told the guy that her husband would be expecting to fuck her when you got home and that she was going to have a hard time hiding the fact that Tony had fucked her so she offered him a hand job instead. It was the same story on the blowjob, but Tony hadn't seen it, only heard about it second hand. I shook my head in amazed disbelief. I never would have expected my wife to go that far to prove something. I knew she was headstrong and that she would go to great lengths to prove a point or win an argument, but to go as far as she had? I guess I didn't know her as well as I thought.

I looked over at Sylvia and found her grinning at me. "There's more," she said. "But you don't get it until after we conclude our arrangement."

This was going to be the first time I had cheated on Leslie and I would have thought that it would have caused me greater inner turmoil than it was. Maybe her fucking Tony was making it easier. I looked at Sylvia and said, "Where do we go from here?"

She laughed and said, "From here we go to my place, sugar."

Her place was a spacious three-bedroom apartment about ten minutes from the café and Sylvia wasted no time when we got there. Once inside the door she turned to face me and said, "No mistletoe here, sugar, we are just going to have to fake it," and she stood on tiptoe and kissed me. It was a hot kiss and when we broke she led me over to the couch and we sat down and started making out like teenagers. We french kissed and groped each other's bodies and it was no different from when I used to take my girlfriends to the drive-in movie.

After five minutes, I had her bra off and had a couple of fingers in her pussy and she had her small fist wrapped around my cock and was pumping it. I finally pulled away from her and said, "We need to move this to the bedroom before I cum in your hand."

She giggled. "That's the idea, sugar. We get the first quick cum out of the way and then we go to the bedroom."

She turned and lowered her mouth and her lips took over from her hands. As her mouth bobbed up and down on my pole I suddenly realized that I was feeling zero remorse at cheating on my wife. In fact, I was enjoying the hell out of it. I pulled Sylvia off my cock and pulled her down to the floor and moved so that I could eat her pussy while she was sucking my dick. Just before her mouth closed around me again I heard her say, "Damn, sugar, I just might have to keep you around for a while."

If her actions were any indication, Sylvia loved having her pussy licked. She pushed herself up at me and started moaning and then she had an orgasm. Her orgasm surprised the hell out of me because she squirted her cum in my mouth. I'd heard that some women could do that but I'd never experienced it. Seconds after Sylvia came, so did I and she swallowed it all. I was beginning to like this girl - a lot! When we separated Sylvia asked, "Do you do that often? Eat pussy, I mean?"

I told her that I did, that Leslie loved it.

"So do I, sugar, but I just can't seem to find men willing to do it. I may have to find some way to hang on to you for a while."

Sylvia led me to the bedroom and we undressed each other. She was just a tad heavy through the hips, but otherwise she was perfect. She seemed to like what she saw and she reached out, took my semi-soft cock and led me over to the bed. It was an active afternoon. We made love three times and between bouts we engaged in sixty-nines. Sylvia was damn near insatiable and I was beginning to wonder if I would be able to leave her place under my own power. We were lying on the bed, breathing heavily, having just finished our third time when she said, "You ready for the rest of it?"

I told her to go ahead and she told me that before the party was over one other black man had gotten her outside with him and he had fucked Leslie while she was bent over the hood of a car. That must have been the man I'd seen follow her out of the ballroom. And then, just before the party broke up Tony had pulled Leslie off into a corner and apologized for his behavior. He said the only reason that he had egged her on was that he had, in fact, thought she was prejudiced against blacks and that it had influenced the way he had acted toward her. He told her he thought that they could be friends and he would like to meet her for drinks and maybe they could talk and get to know each other better.

"Is that all?" I said. "I know about that. Leslie told me that last night."

Sylvia laughed. "Sugar, my brother is the original silver tongued devil," and she looked at the bedside clock, "and right now he is busy sweet talking your wife into spreading her legs for him again. Tony is like most black men. There is something in the back of his brain that makes him want white women. I don't know why, but black men want white women and white women seem to want a black cock at least once in their life. If I know my brother he is going to fuck your wife again tonight and if he does she is going to be in for a wild time for the next month or two."

I rolled up on my elbow and looked at her. "Why is that?"

"Because, sugar, he'll fuck her half a dozen times and then one night he will share her with a buddy, and then two, and by the end of a month she'll be doing gangbangs."

I looked at her like she was crazy. My Leslie doing two guys at the same time? Doing gangbangs? No way!

She saw the look on my face and said, "Oh it will happen, sugar. Her only hope is to not fuck him again, but if he gets her to spread for him tonight it will happen. I guarantee it. Unless of course you stop it before it starts."

I asked, "What do you mean by that?"

"Two things, sugar. You either keep him from fucking her tonight or you tell her what will happen if he does."

I was confused and said, "How do I stop him? I don't even know where they are going for drinks."

She giggled. "Too late for that, sugar. You will have to stop him from putting his chocolate joy stick in her at the scene."

I looked at her with an expression that fairly screamed what the fuck are you talking about. Sylvia laughed and said, "Oh, did I forget to tell you? Tony and I share this apartment and if my brother runs true to form, he should be showing up here with your wife any minute now."

Almost as if on cue we heard the front door slam closed. I jumped out of the bed and grabbed for my pants, but Sylvia grabbed my arm. "Don't panic, sugar. We have rules and one of them is that if the other person's bedroom door is closed, we don't bother that person. Do you want to see if your sweet Leslie is going to be getting some black cock tonight?"

She could see from my face that I was dying to know and she got up and turned out the lights and walked over to her dresser. There was a mirror hanging over it and she took it down to reveal a room through a see through mirror. "This was here when we moved in. I got first pick of rooms and I chose this one. I found this when I went to rearrange the room and the best part is that Tony doesn't know about it. I've seen some pretty wild shit over the last two years."

I looked at her and asked her what she was going to say when he rearranged his room and found it. She laughed. "No way, sugar. He likes to watch himself fuck white bitches and the mirror is in just the right place for him to do it."

We were standing there looking into Tony's bedroom when the door opened and Tony came in carrying Leslie in his arms like a groom carrying his new bride over the threshold. "The only bad thing about this," Sylvia said, "is that there is no sound, you can't hear a thing."

Tony set Leslie down on the floor and went over and pulled down the bed covers while Leslie stripped off her clothes. "No warm up," Sylvia commented. "He must have really gotten her worked up in the bar or in the car."

Leslie walked over to Tony and began undressing him. As soon as he was naked she pushed him back on the bed and knelt between his legs and took his cock in her mouth. "Sure hope she doesn't expect reciprocity," Sylvia said. "Tony doesn't like eating pussy."

I was transfixed as I stood there watching Leslie's red lips and white face slide up and down that black pole. Sylvia said, "Here's your chance, sugar. Go in there and break things up or get used to getting sloppy seconds from your wife."

I didn't even glance at Sylvia, I was too engrossed in watching my wife of fifteen years sucking another man's cock, and a black man at that. Leslie was obviously not a bigot, at least not any more. Tony said something and Leslie got up and lay down on the bed. She spread her legs wide and Tony moved between them. I watched as his black pole slid out of sight into my white wife and then he was fucking her with hard and fast strokes and Leslie's legs came up and locked around him. The sight of her white against his dark was startling and for a while I forgot that it was my wife being fucked in that room. It was like I was watching a porno movie with the sound turned off. I was so wrapped up watching what was taking place in front of me that I hadn't noticed Sylvia dropping to her knees in front of me.

I heard, "My, oh my. He likes watching black cock slide into his lily white wife," and I looked down to see that my cock was indeed hard as a rock and Sylvia's open mouth was on its way to engulf it.

It was weird. I would look down and see my white cock disappear into Sylvia's dark brown mouth and then look up to see Tony's dark brown cock disappear into my white wife. Down, up, down, up and then my hands were in Sylvia's hair and I was fucking her face. She started making choking noises and I let go of the back of her head and started to pull my cock out of her mouth, but she grabbed me and pulled me back and I exploded against the back of her throat. She held me in her mouth and I could feel her throat constrict as she swallowed and gulped down every bit she could squeeze out of me. When I was limp she let my dick fall out of her mouth and she looked at me.

"Why did you do that?"

"Do what?" I asked.

"Try to pull your dick out of my mouth."

"You were choking," I said.

She gave me a strange look and said, "Most men wouldn't have cared. Every other man I've ever known would have grabbed my hair and pushed it in harder and held it there until he came."

I reached down and picked her up. "I'm not most men," and then I kissed her. From the way she acted I guess not many men kissed her after cumming in her mouth. She stepped back and looked at me and then shook her head.

"I've never had much to do with white men and to be honest the only reason I went after you was to get even with her. But I want you to know that I'm glad I fucked you. You are so different from the other men in my life. I'm going to hate not seeing you again."

Back in the other room Tony had finished and he was lying next to Leslie on the bed. Her legs were spread and I could see Tony's cum leaking out of her. She said something to him and then she swung around and started sucking his dick. It took several minutes and then he was hard again and Leslie swung over him and lowered herself onto his cock. I looked at Sylvia and asked, "How many times is he good for?"

She smiled and said, "He can go all night, sugar. The deciding factor here will be what time she has to be home."

I looked at my watch and said, "Have I got time to eat your pussy and still beat her home?"

She smiled and took my hand and led me to the bed.

I fucked Sylvia one more time that night and then I stood in front of the see through mirror while I dressed and watched Tony fuck my wife. I couldn't hear, but from her facial expressions it looked like she was begging him to fuck her harder or faster, or maybe both. Sylvia stood next to me and asked, "What are you going to do?"

"I don't really know," I said. "A lot will depend on what she says and does when she gets home. I suppose it is possible that she will come home and say "Hey babe. Guess what? I just got laid by Tony. Still think I'm a bigot?" but I'm betting that won't happen." I turned to Sylvia and took her in my arms and kissed her. "You told me the other night that you and Tony told each other everything, but this is our little secret, right?"

She hugged me and said, "Anything you say, sugar. Call me?"

I smiled at her and said, "We'll see."

***

I was home in front of the TV when Leslie came home. I looked at my watch and saw that it was almost eight-thirty. She was all smiles and I said, "You obviously had more than a couple of drinks. What did he do? Ply you with drinks and then have his way with you?"

She laughed and said, "No silly. A couple of other people that we knew joined us and we got to talking and lost track of time. Tony was very nice and I think I can learn to like him. I still think he is a little too arrogant, but so what? I have a surprise for you."

I asked her what and she told me that the couple sitting next to them thought that their table cloth was covering them and the woman was stroking the man's cock under the table. "I got so hot watching them that I'm soaking wet and ready to fuck," and she grabbed my hand and pulled me out of the chair. She headed for the bedroom, shedding clothes on the way and I followed along wondering how it was going to play out. I always ate her before I fucked her and I wondered if she was going to let me go down on her while she still had Tony's cum in her. I undressed and got on the bed - moment of truth time - and I lowered my face toward her pussy, but she grabbed me and pulled me on top of her.

"No foreplay, baby, I'm hot enough already. Just fuck me, okay? Make love to me."

Considering how many times I'd watched Tony fuck her that night I was surprised that she didn't feel any different from when I followed myself into her on nights we did it more than once. But mentally it was something else. I couldn't forget that it was that black cock that I'd seen driving into her that was responsible for that sloppy feeling. As I fucked Leslie (I wasn't making love to her that night) I wondered what was going on in her head. Last night, when we'd gotten home from the party, she could have said (as she usually did) that she'd had too much to drink and didn't want to make love. Instead she had been a sex maniac and fucked me almost as much in one night as she usually did in a week.

The same thing this night. Since we had been so active the previous night she could have gotten by with passing tonight, but she was just as horny as she had been following the Christmas party. Did fucking Tony make her hornier, or was she getting a charge out of knowing that I was soaking my cock in another man's cum? I had to admit that I wasn't really sure that I cared. She was hotter than a two-dollar pistol and I loved it. I just hoped that after the afternoon I'd spent with Sylvia that I would be able to stay with her. Luckily, because of the time spent with Sylvia I was a long time in cumming and it seemed like the once was going to be enough for Leslie.

Next morning Leslie woke me up with a blowjob. "I don't know what's come over me. I just can't seem to get enough of you lately. You don't mind, do you?"

The truth was I didn't know if I minded or not. Since the Christmas party, Leslie had turned into a nympho and that part I didn't mind. But what had turned her into a nympho was another man's cock and in my mind that was cheating and I should mind that. Hell, I didn't know what to think.

Over breakfast Leslie told me she might have to work late that night, but she would call me at work and let me know for sure. The day was a fucked up one for me because I could not get the picture of that black cock sliding into Leslie out of my mind. Leslie hardly ever worked late so I was almost certain that Tony was going to be fucking her again tonight. Around one Leslie called me and told me that she would indeed be working late. I told her not to worry, that I had some work that would keep me late also and that she might even beat me home.

"Well, if I beat you home you will find me waiting for you with my legs spread."

"Egad, woman, what has gotten into you lately!"

She chuckled. "You, baby. I haven't stopped thinking of your cock since I left the house."

I stared at the phone for a minute after Leslie hung up and then I picked it back up and dialed a number I had recently memorized. When Sylvia answered I asked, "Would you be willing to let me watch tonight's program on the big screen if I spent a little time before hand licking your pussy?"

I heard her squeal, "Sugar, you sure know how to sweet talk a girl. We will have to be in our seats by six to catch the first show."

That night I was in place and watched Tony fuck Leslie three times. I spent some quality time with Sylvia, but left long before Tony and Leslie finished. If I'd have waited until Tony and Leslie finished I might have run into one of them on my way out of Sylvia's room. I waited down the street until Leslie got home and then I went home. She was in the bedroom undressing when I got there and she gave me a big smile.

"Just in time lover, I need to be fucked."

That night though I was curious to see if she would fight to keep my mouth off her pussy so I went right for it.

"No, baby, no foreplay, I'm hot enough already. Just fuck me, baby, just put it in." I kept going and dragged my tongue along the length of her slit and she moaned, "Oh god, baby, you know I love it when you do that, but just fuck me tonight, please, baby?"

I climbed over her and once again I sank into Tony's soup. Leslie had to "work late" the next two nights, but I didn't call Sylvia to see if I could come watch. Not because I didn't want to, but because between Leslie and Sylvia I was fast wearing out. Each night Leslie would come home hot to be fucked and I did my best to give her as much as she wanted. I was still torn between the two poles tugging at me, cheating bitch on the one side and sexual dynamo on the other, but I couldn't figure what to do about it. I loved her and from her actions when she was around me I believed that she still loved me. If I confronted her would I lose her? Confrontation would definitely alter our relationship in some way, wouldn't it? Did I want to take the chance? I didn't think so. I decided to leave well enough alone and see what would happen.

Sylvia called me at work and asked me to meet her for lunch. As soon as the waiter was gone she said, "What's the matter, sugar? Tired of your little black baby already?"

I smiled and told her not in the least, but that I had to back off before she and Leslie put me in the hospital. She gave me a quizzical look and I had to explain that she and Leslie were fucking me to death.

"You mean to tell me that after Tony does her three or four times she comes home and does you two or three times?" I nodded my head yes. "Damn! I guess I'll have to give her a little more respect."

Our food came and when we had finished eating Sylvia said, "Well, she might cut you some slack tonight, sugar. She might be a little on the tired side when she gets home."

"What does that mean?" I asked.

"Remember I told you that if you didn't stop her, Tony would eventually bring in a friend, and then two and finally your wife would be doing gangbangs?"

I nodded that yes I remembered and she went on, "Well tonight, sugar, is the night that your wife gets two black salamis parked in her. I just thought you would like to know."

It was a no brainer. "What time is the matinee?" I asked.

"Show starts at five-thirty sugar, but the 'box office' will be open at five, if you get my meaning."

I assured her that I did and that I would be there in plenty of time to pay the admission charge. I got to Sylvia's at four forty-five and she met me at the door in all her naked glory. I ate her pussy and then we had an intense bout on the bed before we heard the front door slam at five-thirty. Five minutes later I was watching Tony slide his black cock into Leslie as Sylvia explained to me how the evening would go. Tony would fuck Leslie the first time, get his cock sucked hard again, and then start to fuck her a second time. His buddy Jeff would be standing at the bedroom door and listening. When he heard Leslie moan or begin asking to be fucked harder or faster he would open the door and walk into the room, say "Oops, sorry to bother you," but then he wouldn't leave. He would take out his cock and start playing with it.

"And the next thing you know Tony will have talked your wife into helping the poor guy out. Jeff will walk over and your wife will start sucking his dick while Tony fucks her. Once she gets started there's no stopping. Tomorrow or the next day it will be two friends and the next day three and finally six or seven. In three years, and with over thirty women, I've only seen one get up and leave when Jeff walks in and I've never seen one not come back when they move up to three. Are you sure you are ready for your wife to become a whore for black cock?"

I shrugged. "Her choice," I said.

One the bed Tony was getting his cock sucked and as soon as he was hard Leslie went to mount him, but he pulled her down and climbed on top of her. "Can't be having her where she can just get up and leave, right?" said Sylvia.

I wished I could hear what was being said in the room so I would have some idea of when to expect Jeff, but I couldn't so I just had to watch.

"Sugar, I just can't get over how turned on you get watching that white slut take my brother's black cock. Here, sugar, let me get in front of you and lean my elbows on the dresser."

I knew what she wanted and I slid right into her hot box. On the bed I saw Leslie's legs come up and lock around Tony and out of the corner of my mind I saw the bedroom door open and a man come in. I saw Leslie notice him and her legs unlocked and started to come down, but Tony said something and she closed her eyes and the legs came back up. I watched Leslie's face and I saw her open her eyes, look over at Jeff and then look away again. A minute later they came back to Jeff and then Tony said something and she looked up at him, back at Jeff and then back up to Tony. The next time Leslie looked back at Jeff he had his cock out and was stroking it. Leslie's eyes watched his hands as he beat himself off and then Tony said something and her eyes went up to him and then back to Jeff and they stayed there. A minute later Jeff undressed and walked over to the bed. Leslie's eyes stayed on his cock until it was inches from her mouth and then she looked up at Tony. He said something and her eye's went back to Jeff's cock and then she opened her mouth.

The scene in front of me was incredible: two black dicks inside my white wife and it was driving me crazy. I started fucking Sylvia as hard as I could, never taking my eyes off of the action on the bed. Tony said something and everybody moved. Now Jeff was lying on the bed and Leslie's mouth was working up and down his cock as Tony fucked her from behind. I was mad with lust and I was so engrossed in what I was watching that Sylvia's moans and entreaties were not even registering on me. When I finally unleashed my ejaculation I came so hard that it hurt.

In front of me I saw cum leaking out of the corners of Leslie's mouth and cum leaking out of her pussy as Tony pulled a softening dick out of her. Tony and Leslie fell to the bed, with Leslie lying between both of them.

I became aware of Sylvia moaning, "Oh, baby, oh sugar" and I pulled my attention from Tony's bed back into Sylvia's bedroom. Sylvia was still bent over the dresser and I was surprised to find that I was still hard. Sylvia moaned, "Jesus sugar, you ever going to get enough of watching that white whore get fucked by black poles? You going to let her keep doing it?"

I started to pump slowly into her. "I don't know if it's watching her get fucked by black cock, or just watching her get fucked, but to answer your question I'm not going to stop her as long as you keep letting me come here and watch."

"Just keep doing what you're doing, sugar; that's the price of admission."

On the bed Leslie was still lying between the two men, but now she had gotten her breath back and she had a cock in either hand and was trying to coax them back to life. It would be several minutes before she managed it so I pulled out of Sylvia, turned her around, picked her up and set her on the dresser. Then, much to her delight, I went down on her.

I didn't fuck Sylvia any more that night; I had to save some in case Leslie wanted me when she got home. I doubted that she would, not with all she was getting in the next room. My dick was still hard and Sylvia stood next to me gently squeezing and stroking it as we watched Leslie fuck both men two more times.

"You know I don't like your wife," Sylvia said, "but I have become fond of you and it's obvious that you love the stupid bitch so I'm going to try one more time. You have to put a stop to this. The next time she comes it will be Tony and some other guy; maybe Jeff, maybe someone else. The next time after that it will be Tony and two guys, then three and after that it could be as many as six or seven and from then on it will never be less than five. In about three weeks Tony will get tired of her and he will turn her over to Jeff or one of the other guys and then she will be doing this some other place, not here. And all she will be is a gangbang whore for blacks and not necessarily blacks who are as nice and clean as Tony and his friends. Some of the women who have come through here have ended up on street corners whoring for the guys that gangbang them. That won't happen to your wife because you care for her and she has you to fall back on, but you need to be aware of where this is going."

I heard her out and then I said what I'd said before, "It's her choice. If she tells me about what she is doing we can talk about it. If she keeps quiet it will have to play out the way it plays. I'm not going to say anything that will ruin this for her. She's doing something that she either feels has to, needs to, or wants to and as long as she comes home to me and continues to be a loving wife I'll keep my mouth shut. I will, however, step in and stop things when we get to the point where Tony tries to pass her off to someone else."

Sylvia gave me a long appraising look. "I can't make up my mind as to whether you are a cold hearted bastard or a really great guy where your wife is concerned."

I smiled at her and said, "I can't make up my mind about that either."

I was sitting up in bed reading when Leslie got home. She came into the bedroom and expressed surprise at seeing me still up. "I was afraid that I wasn't going to get my goodnight fuck," she said as she stripped off her clothes. I saw a trace of cum on her inner thigh before she turned and went into the bathroom. I heard the water running and when she came back the trace was gone. She pulled the covers off of me and smiled when she saw my erection.

"I see you've been waiting for me," and she bent over and took it in her mouth - the same mouth that I'd seen wrapped around the black cocks of Tony and Jeff. The remembrance of that white face swallowing those black cocks made my dick twitch and she felt it. "Like this, do you?

Well, that's good because I love doing it to you."

While waiting for Leslie to get home, I'd rethought my stance on what to do and I had decided to confront her tonight. I wanted to pull her into a sixty-nine, but I wouldn't be able to see her face when my tongue touched her freshly fucked cunt. I pulled myself out of her mouth and rolled her on to her back. She opened her legs for me, expecting me to slide my cock into her pussy, but I lowered my face to her cunt. "Don't, baby, just make love to me, okay?"

I kept moving and I stuck my tongue out and poked it at her cunt lips. "Please, baby," Leslie moaned as she put her hands on my head and pushed me away. "Don't do that. Just make love to me, please?"

I looked up at her. "You have always loved my eating your pussy. You've always told me that it's your favorite thing, but you haven't been letting me do it for almost two weeks now. The only reason that I can think of for this is that you have been fucking someone else and you are afraid that I'll taste him if I eat you, is that it? Are you getting some strange cock on the side?"

She just looked down at me so I lowered my head again. Again she pushed me away and I looked up at her and our eyes met and I could see pain in hers and then she turned her head away from me and said, "Yes, I've been fucking someone else."

"Fine," I said. "Now that we have that out of the way, can I please eat the pussy of the woman I love?" I didn't wait for an answer - I just did it.

***

I spent a good five minutes eating Leslie's pussy. It was the first time I'd tasted cum other than mine and to be honest about it I couldn't tell the difference. I brought Leslie to two orgasms before I raised myself up to slide my cock in her.

"What do you want?" I asked. "Should I make love to you, or fuck you?"

She looked me right in the eye and said, "Make love to me, baby. I've already been fucked tonight."

When it was over and we were lying together I said, "Stop me if I'm wrong. Every night you said you were working late you were actually being fucked by another man. That other man has been Tony, and I'm willing to bet that the first time you fucked him was because he more or less dared you to. I'll also bet that the first time you fucked him it was on the back seat of our car."

Leslie sat up and started to say something, but I cut her off, "Let me finish. The next day over drinks he apologized for his behavior, but left you thinking that he still thought you were prejudiced. Determined to prove him wrong you let him fuck you again that evening. What caused the next several times, the knowledge that you were violating the old taboo about white women and black men, or did you actually like being fucked by Tony?"

She was silent for a moment and then she said, "I suppose that it was a little bit of both."

"What I don't understand is your need to come home and fuck me every night after you were fucked by him."

Again silence for a bit and then, "I don't know if you will understand this, but I didn't come home and fuck you. I had just been fucked and I came home and made love to you as a way of cleansing myself. Even when Tony was fucking me my mind was split in two pieces. One piece was the deliciously wicked feeling of forbidden sex and the wanton feeling of just rutting with another man. And the other piece was thinking of coming home and letting you make love to me and having the tenderness and caring that I got from you - two different worlds I guess."

"And tonight, when Tony brought Jeff in to help him?"

I saw the shock register on her face. "You know? You've known all along?"

I looked at her. "I knew before it happened. I could have stopped it at any time, but I love you enough to let you do what you want. I was sure you loved me enough to come home to me, but the next few steps in your sexual transformation could change things so I felt that tonight I had to bring things out into the open."

She gave me a questioning look and said, "What do you mean, my sexual transformation?"

I explained to her the plan that was supposed to turn her into a gangbang whore with the aim of turning her into a streetwalker working for a pimp. She looked at me with a look of incredulity and then she asked me how I knew these things. I explained to her the relationship between Sylvia and Tony and everything that had happened the night of the party and how Sylvia had diverted my attention so the black guys could try and seduce her. I told her how Sylvia had been keeping me informed on everything that had been happening. I didn't tell her about the mirror and that I had been watching, but I did tell her about the way Sylvia felt about her and why and what Sylvia's price for giving me the information was and that I had paid it.

She was quiet and just about the time I thought she wasn't going to say anything, she said, "It's my fault." I looked at her and she said, "It's my fault she feels that way. I should have talked to her and explained why she didn't get the promotion. She was the most qualified and the most experienced, but the company policy manual requires a minimum of one full year of employment before you can move into that position. She only had nine months and the company wouldn't waive the requirement. I know, because I tried to get her one. She will get the next opening, but it's my fault for not telling her all that." She was quiet for a minute and then she said, "Was she good in bed?"

I chuckled and said, "I'm not asking you about Tony, or Jeff for that matter, so I'm not going to answer you on that one."

More quiet and then she said, "I'll get it out of her tomorrow anyway and for your information Tony and Jeff are great fucks. I'm going to miss them. I was having a great time getting all that sex."

I looked her right in the eye and said, "Why are you going to miss it? I'm not telling you to stop, I'm just telling you their plan so you know what you will be getting into. You get to be the one to decide where to draw the line. You can fuck them as much as you want to. All I ask is that you come home to me."

A long look and then she opened her arms. "Make love to me, baby, make love to me."

The next morning I called Sylvia before she left for work. Tony answered the phone and I asked for Sylvia.

"Who's this?" he demanded.

I countered with, "Who are you?"

He responded with, "Don't give me no shit, man, I asked you a question."

"And I asked you one, asshole. When I call my girlfriend and a man answers, I want to know what the fuck is going on. Now who the fuck are you and what are you doing answering Sylvia's phone at this time in the morning?"

There was a moment of quiet on his end and then he said, "I'm her brother Tony."

"Yeah! Like I'm supposed to believe that. She didn't tell me about no brother."

"Hang on," he said, "I'll get her."

There was silence for a minute and then Sylvia came on the line and said hello.

"How is my little black baby this morning?"

"Fine, sugar, hot enough to fuck, but you're not here. What is Tony so wound up about?"

I told her about our conversation. "I thought I'd jerk his chain a little. I'm pissed off at him."

She laughed, "Why? Because he's fucking your wife? I thought that was turning you on. I thought you were getting a major charge out of seeing his black cock plowing that white slut you are married to."

I said, "I'm pissed at him because he was planning on passing her off to someone else. I want my wife treated better than that."

Then I told her the reason for the call, that I'd brought things out in the open and that I'd told Leslie everything except for the mirror. "I told her that I'd only screwed you one time as your price for giving me the information on what she's been doing. She will probably call you in to her office today and I don't care what you tell her, or how you handle it, but please keep the mirror our secret."

She was silent for a moment and then said, "You told her about the plan?"

"I had to, baby. If she wants to go forward with her affair with Tony, she should at least know what she is getting into."

"Wait a minute here," Sylvia said. "You mean she knows that you know and she might still see Tony? Does she care what it might do to your marriage?"

I laughed at that. "She has my permission, baby. She can do

whatever she wants as long as she comes home to me."

I could almost hear her shaking her head in disbelief. "You think she will still come over here with Tony?"

"Don't know. Only time will tell, but if she does I want to be able to watch. Call me and let me know if anything happens this morning. We'll do lunch, okay?"

"You got it, sugar. And sugar?"

"Yeah?" I said.

"I like you a lot better now."

At ten-thirty I got a call from Sylvia and she said she had just left Leslie's office and asked if we were we still on for lunch. We met at the café where we'd had our first meeting and the first thing Sylvia said was, "I don't hate her anymore. In fact I left her office feeling guilty for what I'd helped do to her. She told me why I didn't get the job, showed me the policy and procedures manual where it said I needed a year on the job, and she even showed me the copy of request for a waiver that was denied. I felt real bad about the situation. She apologized for not telling me why I was passed over."

Then Sylvia giggled. "Then she asked me if you had eaten my pussy and I told her that you had and that I'd loved it. Then she asked if I'd like to take you to bed again and when I said yes she said she would work out a way to arrange it. She said it was the least she could do for you considering what you are letting her do. I could learn to like that lady a lot. You two got something I've never seen before. I hope I can find a guy like you, and if I do I'll do my best to be like your wife. But she is still a slut - her words, not mine - and she said she likes being a slut for my brother. Then we talked about Tony and the plan he had for her."

They had talked for almost an hour and the gist of the conversation was that Leslie wanted things to remain as they were. She was willing to go as far as the gangbang, but she wanted to know how to keep Tony from getting tired of her. Then she had asked Sylvia if she was still going to tell me everything and when Sylvia had asked her if Leslie wanted her to, Leslie had said yes and then had said, "I just wish there was some way he could watch." Sylvia had almost told her about the mirror, but then she had remembered that she promised me she wouldn't.

"So," I said. "Does this mean we are on for tonight?"

Sylvia smiled and said, "I guess so, but the price of admission hasn't changed."

I chuckled and said, "I'll gladly pay it, sweetie."

That night I ate Sylvia's pussy twice, once before I fucked her and once after, and then I watched as Leslie got soundly fucked by Tony and Jeff and when she got home I was in bed waiting for her.

"Sweetheart, I hope you don't mind, but I've had so much cock tonight that I don't think I'll be able to fuck you." She saw the look on my face and then she laughed, "So I brought a substitute," and Sylvia walked into the room. Leslie said, "I can't figure out a way for you to watch me so I'm going to watch you."

"Ready for your little black baby, sugar?"

It was a novel experience for me to have Leslie watch me fuck Sylvia and eat her pussy, but I gave it my best shot and then I got to do something really unique - I got to sleep between Leslie and Sylvia. In the morning I woke up with my cock in someone's mouth and I looked down and saw Sylvia working on my dick. When it was hard she turned to Leslie and said, "Your turn" and Leslie swung over me and mounted me. Two seconds later Sylvia sat on my face. God, what a glorious way to start a new day.

I called Sylvia at work around ten and asked her if we were on for that night.

"Not tonight, sugar. I think your favorite slut is going to be coming home early tonight. Sorry, sugar. I was really looking forward to collecting admission. I've fallen in love with that tongue of yours."

"What happened?" I asked.

"You'll have to ask your wife about that, sugar."

"You going to be home around five? I love the way your pussy squirts when you come and I'm willing to let you have some of the tongue you love if you'll squirt for me."

She laughed, "God, but you are one silver tongued devil. I'll be here waiting for you, sugar."

I didn't get home until seven that night and I found Leslie waiting for me. "Didn't expect you to be here so early. Isn't tonight the night you were supposed to be moved up to three?"

Leslie smiled. "I'm changing Tony's plan a little. Sylvia thinks the way to keep Tony from losing interest is to play hard to get, so for the next couple of days you get to be the only one to fuck me. Can you handle it? If you can't there are the other guys from the Christmas party, the hand job, the blow job, and the guy who fucked me on the hood of his car. I think they might like another taste of me, you think?"

I said I'd do my best, but if she needed more to go and get it. "You know my position, baby, you do what you feel comfortable with, just drag yourself home to me."

She laughed. "I just might. The one who took me on the hood of his car had a pretty good-sized cock. And by the way," she said as she took off her clothes. "I'd like it if you were to spend some time with Sylvia, I like that girl and she says she loves the way you eat her pussy and I do feel I owe her something."

"For what?" I wanted to know.

"For keeping you occupied so Tony could fuck me."

I slid my cock into her and said, "While we are on the subject, what's this thing about keeping Tony from getting tired of you? Is there some emotional attachment forming that I should get concerned about?"

She wrapped her legs around me and pulled me down to her. "No silly. It's just that I'm enjoying what we have going right now. If it gets to the point that he tries to push me off on somebody else, I'll have to stop. I have no intention of going anywhere near where Sylvia says I'll end up and I'm not going to go and find someone else when it's over. Now shut up and fuck me."

I smiled down at her and said, "Fuck you? Don't you mean make love to you?"

She gave me a wicked grin and said, "No damn you, I haven't been fucked yet tonight so you have to do it. If you can get it up again after, then you can make love to me."

It was three days before Tony was able to talk Leslie into seeing him again. Over the next two weeks she met with him half a dozen times before she agreed to let Jeff back into the act. When that happened she experienced her first double penetration and watching it made me so hot that I fucked Sylvia so hard that she asked me to take it easy. The fourth week she didn't argue when a third man was added and I watched as the three men did things with Leslie that I would have thought impossible. At one time she had all three of them in her and it drove her wild. That night she didn't fuck them to a standstill, they wore her out. Surprisingly, given the fact that the three men had left her looking like a rag doll, Leslie still wanted my cock when she got home. She did two more nights with the three guys and then she stopped seeing Tony again.

During the same period I was seeing Sylvia on a regular basis and still doing my best to keep up with Leslie's demands, which had slowed down some now that she was fucked by three other guys. Once she stopped seeing Tony again I had to try to pick up the slack and I was starting to have some serious doubts about my ability. It was three weeks before Tony talked her into coming back and on her second night they brought in a fourth man. I watched through the mirror as the four men did all the things that four men could do to a woman, but for some reason it didn't turn me on. It was just too repetitious and with all those bodies around it was difficult for me to even see Leslie and it was seeing her, I realized, that was the turn on. When they were done Leslie was left lying limp on the bed, a cum covered mess, and I wondered if she would be able to get home on her own. Sylvia read my thoughts and told me to go on home and that she would take care of Leslie.

About an hour after I got home, Sylvia came in with Leslie and Leslie gave me a rueful smile and said, "They did me good tonight, baby. I'm going to soak in the tub and let Sylvia tell you all about it. Besides, she likes the price you pay for information."

I woke up with the two women in bed with me, but Leslie begged off and let Sylvia do the honors. Over breakfast I asked Leslie if she was going to keep on. "Last night you were pretty whipped and that was only four guys. How are you going to be able to do a gangbang with six or seven guys there? Maybe it's time to end this little adventure."

Leslie shook her head, "I want to do it at least once. I may have to be carried home, but I do want the experience."

That night Leslie stayed home and we made slow leisurely love several times over the course of the evening and talked a lot about where we were heading. Specifically, about whether she was going to be able to remain a one woman man after her interlude with Tony was over.

"I don't know?" she said. "Are you going to want me to?"

I didn't have an answer for her.

The following morning I got a call from Sylvia telling me that the gangbang was on for that night, "Make sure you don't miss this one, sugar."

I told her that I would be there in plenty of time to pay the admission change and she said, "Sorry, sugar, I can't do that anymore," and she told me that she had started seeing a guy and she liked him a lot. "I can't start out our relationship by having a guy on the side. I'll miss it, sugar, but maybe I can teach him to do it."

Ten minutes later Leslie called, "Tony just asked me if I would mind if he brought several friends over tonight. When I asked how many he said seven. I may be really late tonight, baby, so don't wait up."

That night I was in Sylvia's room waiting when Tony and Leslie came through the bedroom door. They undressed each other, got on the bed and went right to fucking. Five minutes later Jeff and two other guys came in and within minutes Leslie was triple penetrated and while she fought to do justice to the three cocks in her, three more guys came in. I had my cock out and I was stroking myself when Sylvia said, "Here, let me do that" and she took my cock in her hand and began giving me a hand job. I started to say "What about your new boyfriend" when she cut me off.

"See that tall asshole that came in with the last bunch? That's the guy I was going to be true to." She moved in front of me and bent over the dresser. "Fuck me, sugar. You might as well get it because he sure ain't."

On the bed Leslie had three cocks in her and she was facing the mirror. I know it wasn't really happening, but it looked like she was looking right into my eyes and then Sylvia said, "I told her about the mirror this morning."

For the next three hours I never left the mirror as black cock after black cock sank into my wife's every opening and throughout the whole affair Leslie managed to have her body in a position where she could look in the mirror and I know it may sound strange, but it felt like we were sharing the experience. When the seven guys were done with her she was lying on the bed totally spent. I'm not even sure that she was aware of the last man who fucked her. In fact, it was a good bet that she wouldn't be able to get up off the bed and make it home. I was stuck in Sylvia's room until the last guy left the apartment, and Tony climbed into bed next to Leslie and turned out the light. Not that being stuck in Sylvia's room was a bad thing.

It was nine o'clock the next morning, a Saturday, before Leslie got home. She was helped in the front door by Sylvia. "Would have gotten her home sooner, but Tony had to fuck her a couple of times when they woke up."

Leslie said, "Sorry, baby, I've got to go soak in a hot tub so I asked Sylvia to come home with me and take care of you."

That was not the last of Leslie's gangbangs, but she did tell Tony that she would only do one every two weeks or so. For the next year she limited her meetings with Tony and his friends to two and sometimes three times a week. Sylvia eventually met a guy that she liked and I stopped going over to her place to watch Leslie, but Leslie always told me, in detail, what had happened when she got home and made "cleansing love" with me. I did video several of her sessions through the mirror and I watch them at home when she is on one of her nights out. Tony never did get tired of Leslie, but she did eventually get tired of him.

There followed a three-month period when the only cock that entered her was mine. During the next three months Leslie had a few affairs, the most memorable being with the guy who had fucked her on the hood of his car at the party. He liked fucking in semi public places where there was a chance of being seen by passersby and it turned out that it turned Leslie on too. He started to get possessive and Leslie dropped him. She had several very brief affairs with a couple of white guys, but they didn't seem to do much for her.

"It's the taboo thing I guess," is what she said. Not to say that our marriage got boring without a bunch of black cocks chasing after her - she still tried to fuck me to death five or six times a week. Then last night she told me that Sylvia had broken up with her boyfriend and had called and asked if Leslie would like to go "out on the prowl" with her and look for some "fresh meat." Leslie asked me if I would mind and I said no, but I laid a condition on her and that's why I am now in my bedroom closet watching a shiny black cock fucking her lily white body. As an added bonus, I'm watching another black cock fucking Sylvia who is lying on the bed next to Leslie. Both girls know I'm in the closet watching and I know that I am going to have a great time when I come out. I just hope that Leslie likes going out on the prowl with Sylvia because I definitely like being in the closet watching.

~~The End~~

WANT FREE COPIES OF MY BOOKS?
Just visit my blog and download free copies of my books:
<u>awesomeauthors.org/justplainbob</u>

Here is a sample from another story you may enjoy!

JUST PLAIN BOB

BUYING MY WIFE

Adult Erotica

The first thing I did when I got back to my office was get out the Yellow Pages and turn to Investigators and Investigative Services. There were three within two blocks of my office and the first two I called couldn't see me for three or four days but the third one said, "Come on down." As I walked the two blocks to Acme Investigative Services I tried to think of what Hargrove must have been smoking. There was no way that Abby could be having an affair with him let alone be planning on marrying him. We were too happy together. We had a great relationship, but at the same time I couldn't help but feel that something made Hargrove approach me and the best way to find out what it was was to put someone on the case to check things out. Maybe Abby was just a good friend and he misunderstood her feelings. For my own peace of mind I needed to find out what was going on.

I met with Mr. Owen Paulson and filled him in on my meeting with Hargrove. I told him that I seriously doubted that my wife was being unfaithful, but I did need to know what Hargrove was up to. The only times Abby was out of the house were for her Tuesday night book club and discussion group, her Thursday night bridge club meeting and her Saturday morning beauty shop appointment to have her hair done while I played golf with three of my friends. I gave Paulson all the information he asked for regarding Abby and then I gave him a check to get him started. Since it was a Wednesday he told me they would put an operative on Abby Thursday morning when she left the house to go to work and then watch her until the following Tuesday. He told me I could stop by or call him Wednesday for a report.

As I walked back to my office I spent more time trying to figure out what Hargrove was really after. I had absolutely no doubt about Abby's love for me, but I could not figure out for the life of me what Hargrove's angle was.

Abby usually beat me home and when I got home that night she was in the kitchen fixing dinner. She stopped what she was doing, came to me and put her arms around me and kissed me. Dinner and dishes out of the way we curled up on the couch to watch some TV and Abby moved in next to me, put her head on my shoulder and cuddled up next to me. This woman cheating on me? No way!

If you enjoyed this sample then look for **Buying My Wife**.

Also by this Author:

The Prodigal Family: The Abbotts

Watching My Shared Wife

The Waitress and the Runaway Husband

Baiting Mr. Little

Too Hot for Henry

Chuck's Fantasy

The Redhead's Desires

Rescued at Riley's

His Every Fantasy

Open Mike Night

Pursuit for Revenge

Why Does He Do That?

Halloween & Drugs

Tracey

When Rob Met Kari

Becoming a Shared Wife, Vol. 1 –
(Wife Sharing and Other Adventures)

Becoming a Shared Wife, Vol. 2 –
(Hazardous Wives)

Becoming a Shared Wife, Vol. 3 –
(Wives Who Stray)

Her Illicit Adventures

What I Want To Do To Her

Too Fun To Give Up

Creamed

Stepping Out

Hottest Wife

Naughty Wives

Deepest and Darkest

More Than She Can Take

Jennifer's Toes

The More The Sexier

Spice Up

Cyndi

Naughty And Nice

House Of Lovers

Hungry For More

Sweet Revenge

Turning Mommies Wild: The Carriage Tales

Bought And Used

Get Me Off

The Gambler

Gail's Price

***

I REALLY LOVE Reviews!

If you enjoyed this book, please share the love and don't forget to leave a review on Amazon or the site of any other retailer you purchased this book from!

I highly appreciate your reviews, and it only takes a minute to write & post one. I can't tell you how much this means to me!

You'll find the list of all my books on my Author Central page... just in case you'd like to leave a review for other books of mine you've read but didn't have time to leave a review.

*Amazon Author Central – http://www.amazon.com/Just-Plain-Bob/e/B00N3S8FJO

One Last Thing, For Kindle Readers...

When you turn the page, Kindle will give you the opportunity to rate this book and share your thoughts on Facebook and Twitter. If you enjoyed my writings, would you please take a few seconds to let your friends know about it? Because... when they enjoy they will be grateful to you and so will I.

Thank you!

Just Plain Bob
justplainbob@awesomeauthors.org

You may also like the books by these authors:

JACK RYDER

The *Step* *Monster* MILF

TABOO EROTICA

I was still moaning and panting for air as Jane lifted her face away from my still oozing prick. She had her mouth closed, but she had a huge grin on her face as she sat up. Jane winked at me then opened her mouth to show me that her mouth was full of my thick white jism. A little bit of it drooled down her chin and dripped down onto her breasts. Then, she closed her mouth and made a gulping noise as she swallowed it all.

"Damn...that was nasty sexy," I groaned.

"That was yummy," Jane giggled. "Did you like it when I was nasty for you?" She asked it in a sort of naughty tone. She moved forward so my oozing dick was right between her tits. "Next time...maybe I'll fuck you with these tits that you love so much," she added. Jane was mashing her tits back and forth on my cock and the oozing fluid smeared all over her chest.

"That would be a lot better than just jerking off when you think about them, Huh?" she taunted me.

"Oh Yes, Jane...Oh God yes, God yes," I moaned. It thrilled me that Jane knew that I think about her when I jerk off. She moved forward and we kissed passionately for several moments. I was surprised that the saltiness of my jizz in her mouth did not bother me one bit.

I had started fondling and squeezing on Jane's cum slick tits while we were kissing. When she finally moved back after the kiss, I pulled her forward and began to suck on her tits greedily. "Oh Peter...Ooouoh Peter," she purred. Jane's hands grabbed my head and she mashed my face harder into her chest. "Yes baby, Ooooh yes," she moaned. I felt her body shudder as I gently bit down on one of her nipples and then pulled on it so it stretched forward. "Ooooh Peter, Yesss, Yesss," she gasped.

I repeated this several more times over the next several moments on both of her nipples. "My pussy is so fucking wet," she moaned throatily. I was pleased to find that her panties were completely saturated with her juice when I slipped my hand between her legs and rubbed my palm against the crotch of her panties. "Oooooh Peeeeeeter," she moaned when I rubbed my fingers up and down her gash.

I pushed Jane's dress up to her waist then ripped her panties down to her feet. "I'm going to fuck you, Jane." I was surprised by the deep lust in my voice as I tossed her panties on the floor.

"Oh, Peeeeeter," she gasped again when I shoved my face against her cunt and started slurping at her dripping sex hole. "Yes Peter...Yes, Yes," she groaned. I could feel her body quivering as I greedily drilled my tongue in and out of her gash. "Oooh Yes, Oooh Yes, Oooh Yes," she wailed.

My dick was fully erect within a few minutes and I was sex drunk from the intoxicating scent of her muskiness. I scooted forward and shoved my 8 inch prick into her hole till I was completely buried in her pussy.

"Ooooooh, Peeeeeeter!" It was a deep husky primal sort of moan. I held myself buried inside of her for several moments to enjoy this first time of being inside my step mother's cunt.

The sloppy wetness of her pussy was exquisite as she trembled beneath me. I could feel Jane's pussy contracting around my prick and every pulsation of my dick inside of her. "Oooh, Jane," I gasped. I had to smile as I remembered saying that as I emptied my balls inside of Sara's tight virgin cunt.

"You feel so fucking good," Jane moaned softly. "Take me, Peter. Fuck me," she moaned in that deep husky voice again. I pulled my dick almost all the way out and slammed it back in forcefully. "Oh my God yes," she bellowed.

Squish, squish, squish, squish...Jane's pussy was so drenched that her juice squirted out all over each time I thrust into her. Because I had already came in Jane's mouth, I was able to fuck her savagely for nearly twenty minutes. By the time I was ready to climax, Jane was so winded from her long series of orgasms, that she suddenly went limp beneath me as she passed out for a couple of seconds.

I was just at the verge of my climax when Jane passed out. When she went limp, her bladder let loose and she wet herself just as my dick began to spasm inside of her. The sloppy sensation of her urine gushing out of her thrilled me so much that my cock absolutely exploded into Jane's quivering womb. My dick squirted four huge wads of cum deep into her womanhood. "Yes, baby, give it to me," Jane moaned softly as she felt my cum flooding into her.

"I'm never going to forget this night," I whispered as I leaned forward and kissed her cheek.

"That is so sweet that you will remember our first time," she whispered back.

"And it was my very first blow job and the first time I ever ate pussy," I informed her softly.

"Oh Peter, I will remember that too, baby." Then she pulled me down and kissed me very passionately.

When we got up off the couch, there was a huge urine stain in the middle of the sofa cushion and globs of cum that oozed out of her gash. Jane pulled her dress off over her head and tossed it on top of the mess. "I'll clean that up tomorrow before your dad gets home," she giggled. I felt elated when she held my hand and led me to her bedroom completely naked. But I also felt sad that my asshole father would be returning just as this was beginning with Jane.

"I'm sorry that I hated you," I whispered in her ear when we were in the bed.

"Don't be silly," Jane chuckled. "You never hated me at all." I could see a genuine love in her eyes as she peered into mine. "You were just trying to block what you really wanted from me." Her fingers were now brushing up and down my chest. "What happened tonight is what you really wanted all along." She leaned forward and kissed my cheek. "I was just waiting for you to figure it out," she added.

"How did you know all of this?" I asked her softly.

Jane just laughed cheerfully. "Because I've heard you jerking off in your room almost every day after you stare at my tits," she giggled. "I heard you moan my name and I found my panties that you used to jerk off on." My face was now turning red. "And I saw you masturbating when you watched me in the shower too," she informed me.

My face was now beet red as she continued to gaze into my eyes. "But that's okay, baby," she chuckled. "I left those panties for you to find and I left the door open so you could see me naked in the shower," she told me softly. "Truth is...I masturbated for you too, baby," she whispered. "My pussy got so wet when you looked at my tits that I would go finger myself as soon as you left the house every morning," she confessed. "So, I decided to try something...to attract your attention." She kissed my cheek. "This was better than I ever dreamed," she whispered.

It felt wonderful as we laid there and cuddled. Jane gently stroked my back as I kissed her neck and chest tenderly. "I think...I could fall in love with you, Jane..."

If you enjoyed this sample then look for **The Step Monster MILF**.

MFF Bisexual Threesome Romance
She Made Him
Do It
Nicki Homewood

After a hundred metres or so they came to a pier that struck out from the riverside ten metres or so into the river itself. It was unlit and disappeared into the blackness of the river, the glare from the streetlights barely reaching the end of it. When they initially arrived it seemed very dark and forbidding, but their eyes quickly adjusted to the gloom.

Rob had an idea and took Natalya by the hand, leading her away from the footpath and right to the end of the pier. She walked up to the steel railings at the end and looked down at the black depths of the river running beneath their feet.

There were very few people walking along the footpath, and the lighting meant that even as they walked past the end of the pier, they would hardly be able to see anything of couple on the pier.

Rob stood behind Natalya and surrounded her, putting a hand onto the railing on either side of her. He pressed himself into her bum, feeling his erection grow in anticipation of what he was planning.

He moved his hands down to her dress and gently pulled it up until the hem was level with her waist. He calculated that her jacket was still hanging down in either side to protect her dignity to some degree but from the opposite bank she would be completely exposed.

He lowered his hand to her button and started to gently massage it, gratified that he could feel she was already aroused, her lips wet with her juices, demonstrably wanting him.

He decided that he would see if he could first give her an orgasm standing there on the pier, and turned his full attention to her oyster, playing with it with both fingers, moving them up and down with focused attention.

Natalya had been shocked when he had first pulled up her skirt; she knew in the back of her mind that her jacket made it difficult for anyone on their side of the river to see anything, but it did not alter the fact that she was standing in the centre of London with her entrance completely exposed to anyone on the river bank north of them.

Quickly though, the insistent movements of Rob's fingers seduced her body into arousal and acceptance. She tensed her legs, eager to feel the satisfaction of him finishing her.

When she finally came, it was with a light scream, only just audible to anyone walking along the footpath. For a moment they both relaxed, their breath quickening. Neither one of them was satisfied though, and immediately Rob unzipped his fly and pulled his pole free from its enclosure. He had been aroused to some degree for a long time, as Natalya had been wearing so little, but now was utterly ready.

"Do me," was the simple command that Natalya uttered at this point, both willing and desperate in its tone.

Needing no such invitation, Rob lifted the back of Natalya's jacket where it hung down over her bum. With his fingers he reached round and pulled her lips wide open, feeling the hard tip of his shaft ready to enter her.

Natalya shifted her pose a little, moving her feet slightly apart and leaning a bit forward onto the railings. Almost immediately she felt him slide swiftly up inside her, as once again she screamed out into the night.

"Do me hard," she insisted again, unnecessarily—even as she said the words, Rob had moved his hands down to her hips and was pulling himself deeper than ever into her.

They were both lost in the moment by this time, oblivious to their central London situation, oblivious to the other couple that was watching them from the bank just behind them.

Rob leaned forwards and placed his fingers back on Natalya's button, resuming his swift but gentle ministrations, sometimes touching the side of his shaft as it slipped in and out of her.

They were utterly shocked however when just a few metres away, two fellow revellers arrived next to them. Rob noticed them first and immediately stopped his movements, Natalya turned to see why and then also realised the proximity of the intruders. They both stood up straight, but Rob remained stock still, his heart racing, his length still firmly ensconced deep inside her.

Their minds raced—what should they do—was it better just to stay there until the other couple went, or to cut their losses and run? They remained transfixed until suddenly it became clearer what was going on.

The other couple was also involved in a deeply sexual adventure, her arms were around his shoulders and she was kissing him deeply and passionately. His hands were roaming all over her, running down her dress from her shoulders, over her breasts down to her entrance.

Almost with the appearance of coordinated thought, he suddenly pulled up the dress, exposing her shaved beauty clearly to Rob and Natalya, and she undid his trousers and took his length in her hands.

His meat was not as long as Rob's, but what it lacked in length it made up for in girth, and as Natalya looked back at it, she wondered what it would feel like to have such an implement pressed hard into her.

Rob could feel his own penis almost explode with arousal as he watched the strangers as she backed into the railings. The guy lifted her with his hands under her thighs and then lowered her down onto his pole. She screamed out with pleasure as he entered her and within seconds was panting with glee as he moved back and forth in and out of her.

Rob resumed his own movements, his feeling twice as sensitive as it slipped in and out of Natalya's sopping slit. Neither couple was able to focus entirely upon themselves, and all of them remained entranced by watching what the other couple was doing. Natalya was suddenly dissatisfied with her position looking away from the scene over the

Thames. She pulled herself away from Rob and felt his length disengage from her, and then bounce into her bum, wet against her skin.

She wanted to enjoy the absolute licentious nature of the moment and decided to see whether the other couple was as bold as they seemed. She turned to face Rob, letting him see her lightly trimmed pubes, now sodden with their essence. She then discarded her jacket, placing it carefully on the railings next to them. This left her standing on the darkened pier, her lace dress pulled up to expose everything below her navel, and her nipples formed into hard cones, poking at the lace.

She took Rob by the hand and then walked towards the other couple and smiled at them as they both watched her wearily, obviously wondering what she would do next.

If you enjoyed this sample then look for **She Made Him Do It**.

KERRY JAMES
HISTORICAL ROMANCE

TIME ONCE MORE *for*
MARILYN
CAPTIVATED & REKINDLED

Nineteen-fifty-seven was not a particularly notable year for the world, or for the inhabitants of the United Kingdom. Of course, there were quite a few people who would look back and say. "That was a good year, a very good year." But for many it was just another year. There were births, quite a few into poverty and starvation and the law of averages dictated that an equal number died possibly from that same poverty and starvation. In October the Soviets would launch the first orbiting satellite and the word 'Sputnik' became part of every language. This was a shock for every developed nation, particularly the Americans, as no one thought that the Russians had the technology to achieve that feat. We all got a year older, although some, like my mother celebrated her birthday and resolutely remained thirty five, ignoring the fact that she was born in nineteen eleven. The Spartan existence, we had known in these isles during WW2 and immediately after had relaxed and our family along with many others was enjoying a more comfortable life.

Our Prime Minister had told us we were never having it so good. At that time, in our innocence we tended to believe the politicians; later the scales would drop from our eyes. For the moment we went along with this fantasy. Most families had a television now and a refrigerator and if those were the yardstick by which to judge then we were indeed better off. There were jobs for all those who wanted to work and State Benefits for those who declined that activity. The Unions flexed their muscles to introduce socialist principles into Industry. They battled for those whom they called 'the workers' implying by inference that anyone who wasn't unionized was a shirker or a parasite or both. The 'workers' ironically spent more time not working; as their shop stewards frequently called them out on strike for the flimsiest of reasons. The Unions espoused democracy yet rarely let their members vote on strike action. The conflict between the workers and the management was a running battle that went on and on, ensuring years later the almost complete demise of British industry. If we were having it so good, it was a Fool's Paradise. However, for the moment we basked in the sunshine.

It was a surprise, therefore when my dad announced that the family was going away for a week's holiday. The surprise was that I was included. When I was young, we had family holidays. A week or two in the West Country, travelling there by train with accommodation provided by the euphemistically described 'Guest House'. A Guest House was one very small step above a boarding house. The furnishings were better, but the rules were the same, whatever the weather you had to leave during the day and not return before five o'clock. You were provided with bed, breakfast, and an evening meal, no early morning or afternoon tea. For me, the journey by train was the highlight. We travelled by 'The Cornish Riviera Express', the crack train of the Great Western, which, in nineteen forty-eight became the Western Region of British Railways. In those days it was still hauled by a steam engine, either a 'King' or 'Castle', gleaming in Brunswick Green with brass trim and copper burnished all glittering in the light. It was supposed to run non-stop to Truro in Cornwall, but it did stop at Plymouth. Not in the station, but just outside so the engine could be changed. The 'Kings' and 'Castles' were too heavy for the Royal Albert Bridge over the Tamar so they were changed for another, lighter locomotive. It was only later that I understood that during the holiday season there were at least three or four trains that left Paddington in the space of an hour and a half, all called 'The Cornish Riviera Express'. That did mar a little the pride in travelling on that special train. In the mid-fifties, my dad took a new job; moving the whole family from the London area to the Midlands. His position also allowed him a company car for private as well as business use. So the romance of the Cornish Riviera was now history.

For three or four years prior to this, my parents had taken advantage of the burgeoning package holiday offers, and would go off to Spain or Italy with my younger sister. I was left at home with a cash bribe from my father to ensure that I would eat properly for the two weeks they were away. I didn't think they were rejecting me; it was probably because they didn't know what to do with an early teenager at the time. Now it would seem that at eighteen, I was acceptable company once more. Those last three years had transformed me from a gangling strip of a boy at five feet six, into a relatively decent looking man of five foot ten with dark brown hair and a face that could be described as reasonable rather than handsome.

The hotel was quite large with most of the amenities that you would expect. It was situated on a promontory called Daddyhole Plain and overlooked the sweep of the bay and the town. I assumed from the look of the place that it had once been the palatial home of some rich man and had been converted into a hotel with extensions for bedrooms and function rooms. The conversion had been done piecemeal so finding your way about was somewhat difficult as corridors seemingly leading in the right direction would take a sudden turn and take you to a place you didn't want to be. My parents and my sister had rooms on the first floor where the best rooms were. My sister got one of those so they could keep an eye on her she was only eleven at the time. I had a single room on the third floor. I got there by taking the main staircase up to the first floor, walking down the long corridor, then climbing another, less grand staircase to the second where I had to reverse the walk on the first floor to yet another, even smaller staircase that would take me to my floor. The room had a quaint ceiling, sloping within the confines of a gable. From the window I had an interesting view over the roofs and back gardens, but not a glimpse of anything remotely like a beach or sea. There was a wash basin with hot and cold running in the room, but for any other needs I would have to go down the corridor. The concept of en-suite facilities was unknown to the majority of hotels in the UK. That changed eventually with dire consequences for those hotels that didn't adapt. I didn't mind the disparity in accommodation; I got some privacy to indulge whatever my teenage hormones could discover for me. As it happened, I didn't have to go looking; adventure in the shape of the female variety came looking for me...

If you enjoyed this sample then look for Time Once More For Marilyn.

Leon Randall

Naughty Mojo

WILD AND SEXY EROTICA

It took only a few seconds to get off the main beach and into the scrubby bushes behind. My 'new friend' whom I was dreading meeting had seen us make our decision to follow and had moved several yards further ahead as we approached. Maybe thirty seconds after that (I had lost my sense of time, anyway) as we followed I was hoping the ground would swallow me. But it didn't, and we met up with him as he waited in a little sandy clearing, stopping a few feet apart. Then he greeted us.

"Hello. It is nice to meet you both. I am Anton." He had a well-modulated voice with a mid-European lilt, where "is" sounded more like "eeze". This quite ordinary, non-confronting greeting quite disarmed my panic, or perhaps sneaked past it, and I found myself responding with part of my brain essentially on automatic pilot while another part couldn't help but have a sense of the surreal.

"Yes, hello. Nice to meet you, too. Um..., I'm Jan and this is Larry." After a moment's pause, I added because of habit, but for no especially useful reason, "My husband."

Larry was holding my hand as we stood there in the little clearing, probably looking like startled, nude statues. Anton looked much more relaxed than I felt, with his towel draped over one arm, as he went on. "Thank you for introducing yourselves by name. People do not always do that."

"That's OK," said Larry, probably being as mystified as I was at the remark. I shrugged as if to indicate it was no big deal.

"I have not seen you here before," Anton continued.

"It's our first visit," I said. "The beach is lovely. Do you come here often?" As those banal words left my lips I was acutely conscious that I didn't know what to say in this weird situation. Fortunately I didn't need to, as the conversation flowed ahead following Anton's lead.

"Yes, it is a favourite place for me." Again, the 'eeze' pronunciation struck me. "Sometimes I meet my friends here. Sometimes I make new friends. It is a friendly place."

"It seems to be," Larry contributed, but then stopped, taking the conversation no further.

Anton paused and making a sweeping gesture that took in everything and nothing at the same time said, "Perhaps you are here also for the pleasures?"

"Pleasures?" I responded, lamely, with what must have been a quizzical look on my face. The way he said 'the' pleasures was quaint but mystifying for a few more seconds until I got the drift of his hint.

"Yes, some people come here for pleasures with others. Before, on the sand, as I watched you, it was a pleasure. Thank you."

I had been a bit slow to catch on, but at that moment I suddenly 'got it'. This was what visitors to this beach do when they come here for exactly what Larry and I had come for. They either know each other already or look for hints and signals before sounding each other out in just this way. As this was sinking in, Anton added, "Perhaps you and your husband want to share pleasures? It is quite customary here."

Yes. There it was. An invitation to do what we had planned for but didn't really think (or, at least, I didn't) would actually happen. Larry, who gave every indication of not having 'got it' yet was no help, saying, "Errr, ummm…"

I was unsure of what to say next myself and must have looked flustered when Anton continued, "I see I may have offended or mistaken you. If so, I apologise. Perhaps you would prefer….."

He was probably going to say that he should withdraw when I found my voice and confidence. It struck me that this seemingly very nice (and, I must say, attractive) man had done nothing that he should apologise for. On the contrary, he really was shaping up to be quite charming. I suddenly felt that I was the one who should apologise to him for the fact that he now felt at a disadvantage he didn't deserve. He had sent out a 'signal' which I had responded to and, in fact, encouraged.

"No, no. Not at all," I found myself saying. "Larry and I are not offended, are we honey?" Being so far unimpressed with Larry's verbal contribution to this whole situation, and him being fairly light on impromptu repartee at any time, I pressed on without waiting for him to reply. "We thought there might be some 'pleasures' as you put it and, well....." I paused there, embarrassed, then thought to myself, Oh-what-the-hell, before finishing bravely, "That's one of the reasons we came here."

There. I'd said it. At that moment I wasn't sure whether I was pleased with myself or terrified of what I may have started. Both, I think. Anton smiled broadly. "That," (it came out as 'zat'), "is very good. Perhaps we could share the pleasures." I wasn't sure if that was a statement or a question.

I looked squarely at Larry for the first time since we had entered this little scrubby clearing, and he looked back at me. As I raised my eyebrows in an unspoken "Well, what do you think?" gesture, at last he mentally caught up with where Anton and I had arrived some thirty seconds ago.

"You mean…?" he said, then trailed off. He didn't need to finish the sentence. I knew that he knew what the question was, and what the answer was, and he knew that I knew he knew. It's like that when you've been married for as long as we have. "Sure, that'd be great," he managed at last, adding "if you're OK with that, Darl."

I am surprised now, looking back, that actually I *was* OK with it; that my initial panic had faded. Anton didn't seem threatening. In fact, quite the opposite, with a quiet charm of manner that was engaging. There was no question he was physically attractive and having overcome my initial fright at the unfolding situation, I remembered with a flash of lust what Larry and I had fantasised about. I also recalled, as I stood there naked in that scrubby clearing, those couple of minutes of heart-thumping turn-on I had experienced as I watched and flirted with this stranger only a short time ago.

Arriving at a 'Hell, why not?' decision wasn't to say that I had a clue what to say or do next, or what I would or wouldn't do next, or what he and Larry would or wouldn't do next, or would want me to do next. Anton again took the lead, and charmingly so, putting me at ease.

"At this beach, the woman, she is always in charge of the pleasures," he said. "It is for you to say."

Despite my bravery in getting this far, I was quite unprepared about how to answer that. I looked once more at Larry who again was no help when Anton continued quite effortlessly and without seeming embarrassment.

"Some couples like others to watch them take pleasures. Jan? Larry? Perhaps this is what you want?"

I was pretty pathetic in my response as I heard myself saying, "Well, yes, that sounds OK, I suppose. What do you think, Larry?"

Now that he was fully tuned-in, Larry said, "Yeah, I guess that would be fun," squeezing my hand which he was still holding.

I was excited but apprehensive. What I definitely didn't want was to have Anton presume I was a shared "pleasure" for both men to have. That wasn't part of Larry's or my mental agenda and I suddenly found myself flustered all over again. By luck, practice or intuition, I don't know which, Anton read my mind and saved the moment. "Jan, do not be concerned. The woman, she is always in charge here," he repeated. "It will be my pleasure to see your pleasure. I need nothing more."

I think at that moment both Larry and I felt quite strange. This was certainly a new scene for us and whilst we had discussed and, I admit, fantasised about exactly this opportunity, to be watched, we both felt awkward about what to do right now that the moment had come. It wasn't as though there was another couple to blend in with, or whose lead we could follow. It was just us, a couple of would-be exhibitionists who had now the chance to follow through or be sorry what they had wished for. Larry was, as he told me later, still a little shell shocked that somehow (and, at the time, he still didn't really know how) we had fallen into this situation and was giving a good impression of being an indecisive, naked dork. But, as I said, he's my dork, and I love him, so I just kissed him. Smack full on the mouth and, pulling back and looking into his face said, "Ok, Mister, if you're in the mood, so am I."

He smiled, and I kissed him again. He kissed me back with some enthusiasm and as I put my arms around his neck he put his around me, both palms resting on my bottom, pulling me in close. "God, you're a sexy creature," he breathed into my ear as we broke the kiss, adding, "I'm beginning to enjoy this."

I glanced towards Anton, who was smiling at us only a few feet away, and who said, "You are an attractive couple. Please.... enjoy."

It's hard for me to recount all the details of what happened in the next few minutes in that little, sandy, scrubby clearing just back from the beach on that sunny, amazing, somewhat frightening but exciting afternoon. I remember it mostly as a blur of eroticism and, yes, plain lust, certainly ranking with the most excitingly sexual, erotic experiences of my life. To my pleasant surprise, I didn't feel unsafe at all. Larry, my lovely dorky but lovable Larry, was there with me. Anton obviously wasn't an axe murderer; just a guy wanting to enjoy some 'pleasures' with others who wanted to share theirs. So, it was that I found that it doesn't take long, only a few tens of seconds indeed, for sexual arousal to set aside inhibitions. Having made up my mind to do this, I was going to enjoy it, have Larry enjoy it and make it quite a show for our new acquaintance.

Unclasping my hands from behind Larry's neck, I squatted down in front of him, put one hand behind his buttocks and with the other, guided his pretty-deflated penis into my mouth. I think it took him by surprise, but I interpreted his sudden "Oh, God, Jan," as encouragement. He told me later he was embarrassed to look at Anton at that moment, but put his hands gently on the back of my head as encouragement. Larry is usually not that quick to get hard, but perhaps the situation or perhaps prior unrequited events in the water contributed to him getting hard, I should say very hard, in less than a minute of my oral attention. It's funny looking back - as I say, it is a blur - but I don't think that, as I was sucking Larry to erection, I was actually thinking about Anton at all.

Once he was impressively erect, I popped him out of my mouth and stood up, kissing him again. One of Larry's hands found my breast, massaged it, then tweaked the nipple while the other hand was busy stroking my side. I had gone from zero to fully turned on in what must have only been a couple of minutes and nearly collapsed when Larry took his hand from my breast and moved it down to my pussy, rubbing my lips and slipping a finger across my clit and then inside.

If you enjoyed this sample then look for **Naughty Mojo.**

Amy Redek

THE GOOD
TWELVE

12 STORIES
IN ONE

My father passed away about a year ago and so I was now alone in my house for my mother had walked out from us many years ago when I was only a child of five. The reason for that my father told me later, was because of him being caught getting another woman pregnant. After an awful row, she had left us, leaving father to raise me on his own.

It was disappointing not to have my mother around but he looked after me well enough in seeing that I was brought up properly. He often took me fishing on the river that ran past the bottom of our garden where we had a boathouse that held our small boat. I say boathouse though it was not a proper one but more of a large shed that covered a small inlet into our garden.

The river was called the Pax and our house was on the outskirts of the town of Paxham, having taken its name from the river when it was just a small hamlet. The boat, which I never did know what type it should be called, was quite deep in the middle and had a small outboard motor attached. I liked this boat because of the inside depth of it for when I took my girlfriend out in it for fishing, it was easy for us to lie down in the bottom of it for us to kiss and cuddle and not be seen when anchored out in the middle of the river.

There was one particular spot about a mile and a half down river where for a stretch of at least fifty yards on either bank, gorse bushes came right down to the river's edge and so it was unlikely that persons on the banks could get down to the river and see my boat anchored and us kissing there.

On this particular day, I was now twenty-six years of age and my girlfriend, Josie, was twenty-one. I loved our kissing of each other and found the courage to ask if she would marry me. I was over the moon when she said yes. I then saw that it was time to return to our houses and so began to pull up the small light anchor that had held the boat still in the slowly moving river.

'It's caught on something,' I said, having difficulty in upping the anchor and she moved to the bow to give me a hand. With both of us pulling on the anchor's rope, it slowly began to come up but we didn't get it out of the river. For as we slowly gathered the rope in we found what it had caught and Josie gave out a scream and we both let go of the rope to sink back down with what the anchor had attached itself to, for we had seen the head of a skeleton!

'Christ Almighty,' I had exclaimed, turning round to hold a shaking Josie and calm her down at her having seen what had once been a living person. What I then did was to get the empty bottle of water he still had in the boat and tied this to the anchor rope that I had cut free and let it float on top of the water to show where this skeleton was.

It was a silent pair that was in the boat as I got the engine running and moved it back upstream to my house where, after mooring the boat, phoned the police to tell them of what we had found. About an hour later, I was being interviewed by two police officers, one of them being a woman, and knew both of them as they were locals like me. They said that after they had got hold of a diver and a boat, they would collect me to show them where in the river I had anchored, which they did.

So with them collecting me, and with their boat being more powerful than mine, we're soon down where I had anchored and found the floating bottle. Now the diver went over the side and two minutes later was back up and confirmed that there was indeed a skeleton anchored below by what looked like a roadside grating. This was confirmed after they had recovered the remains of which I had no part for they had left me behind when they did this later in the day, but was told of this the following day when I gave a full statement down at the local nick.

Two divers had gone down, one to lift the skeleton and one the grating that was chained to the legs. Between them, they got both to the surface where others took over to get them into the boat where they were taken to the town for an autopsy. I queried this word asking how can you do an autopsy on a skeleton? I thought that it had to have flesh for this to be carried out but was told that bones could still be identified by any bone marrow left, the pelvic bones and teeth. They guessed that it could be somebody local for the grating was of the same style as that used in the town to drain off the rain water from the roads.

Well the pelvic bones told them that it was of a female and they could also start checking with the teeth because of the possibility of it being a local woman and these teeth being noted at some dentist's records. It took a few weeks but they found a match which shocked me, for the woman's name was Joan Redmond. I haven't told you yet that my name is Jack Redmond and this was most likely the bones of my mother that I had hooked onto.

I was in shock!

Could this really have been my mother who was supposed to have walked out from our home twenty one years ago? There was only one way to find out and agreed for them to do a D.N.A. test on me to see if it was a match to the bones of the woman. This didn't take long to confirm that there was a match and it was indeed that of my mother.

Now this raised another question, apart from the fact that my father must have murdered her, though how, they couldn't say, and chained her legs to the grating and dumped her there and put out the story that she had left him because of him getting another woman pregnant. When the news broke out in the town, the question came from the mother of Josie who claimed that it was my father, John Redmond who had gotten her pregnant and therefore requested that Josie went through D.N.A. testing to compare it with mine.

If you enjoyed this sample then look for <u>The Good Twelve.</u>

WANT FREE COPIES OF MY BOOKS?
Just visit my blog and download free copies of my books:

awesomeauthors.org/justplainbob

www.ingramcontent.com/pod-product-compliance
Lightning Source LLC
Chambersburg PA
CBHW071415170626
46811CB00003B/1411

* 9 7 8 1 6 8 0 3 0 5 1 2 8 *